Discovering Emily

Jacqueline Pearce

ORCA BOOK PUBLISHERS

Copyright © 2004 Jacqueline Pearce

All rights reserved. No part of this publication may be reproduced or transmitted in any form or by any means, electronic or mechanical, including photocopying, recording or by any information storage and retrieval system now known or to be invented, without permission in writing from the publisher.

National Library of Canada Cataloguing in Publication Data

Pearce, Jacqueline, 1962-
Discovering Emily / Jacqueline Pearce.

(Orca young readers)
ISBN 1-55143-295-1

I. Title. II. Series.

PS8581.E26D58 2004   jC813'.6   C2004-904720-5

Library of Congress Control Number: 2004110935

Summary: At the age of eight, Emily Carr struggles to develop her artistic ability within a strict family and in a conservative time.

Free teachers' guide available.

Orca Book Publishers gratefully acknowledges the support for its publishing programs provided by the following agencies: the Government of Canada through the Department of Canadian Heritage's Book Publishing Industry Development Program (BPIDP), the Canada Council for the Arts, and the British Columbia Arts Council.

Typesetting and cover design by Lynn O'Rourke
Cover & interior illustrations by Renné Benoit

In Canada:	**In the United States:**
Orca Book Publishers	Orca Book Publishers
1016 Balmoral Road	PO Box 468
Victoria, BC Canada	Custer, WA USA
V8T 1A8	98240-0468

07 06 05 04 • 6 5 4 3 2 1

Printed and bound in Canada.
Printed on 100% post-consumer recycled paper,
100% old growth forest free, processed chlorine free
using vegetable, low VOC inks.

*For my good friend, Jean-Pierre,
who has shared an interest in art
with me since we met in grade two;
for my daughter, Danielle,
who also likes to draw and paint;
and for all you readers who love art.*

Table of Contents

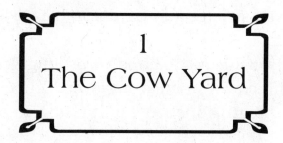

1
The Cow Yard

"It's so unfair!" Emily grumbled as she stood inside the cow yard fence, scratching the stiff hair on top the cow's head.

She glanced back at the house and scowled. All she'd done was slide down the banister and maybe sing out a bit as she sailed down. How was she to know that her oldest sister, Dede, was entertaining church ladies in the drawing room? Emily fumed at the memory of the scolding Dede had given her in front of the visitors. She could never do anything right in Dede's eyes. When Mother wasn't feeling well and Father was at work, Dede was in charge, and she took the job seriously. Dede, whose given name was Edith, was fifteen years older than Emily. Sometimes it seemed she was even stricter and harder to please than Father.

Emily held out a handful of long grass, and the cow munched it slowly. The cow's warm breath touched Emily's fingers, and her big dark eyes seemed to regard Emily sympathetically. The chickens pecked in the dirt near Emily's feet, making their soothing clucking sounds. Emily sighed. She always felt better after visiting the cow yard. She picked up a stick and began drawing in the dirt. Lazy circles began to take the shape of the cow.

When she was smaller, Emily and her youngest sisters, Alice and Lizzie, had often played together in the cow yard. They'd visited the animals, fished for tadpoles in the pond and sailed paper boats down the little creek. But first Lizzie, then Alice, had tired of the cow yard. It was too dirty for them now. They liked to keep their frocks clean and pretend to be proper ladies. Emily had no interest in sitting around being a lady. She would much rather be a farmer's wife, with lots of animals to take care of, or a circus horse rider who jumped through hoops of fire.

Emily looked over at the flower garden in front of the house where Alice and Lizzie were playing with dolls. Alice would be the mother, as usual, while Lizzie was probably pretending to be a missionary, quoting the Bible to everyone. Lizzie looked up.

"Milly!" she called, using the shortened name the family often called Emily. "Come out of there before you dirty your frock. Father will be home soon."

Emily turned her back on Lizzie. How dull playing at ladies was. She set down her stick and gazed at the cow. She was no horse, but she was the right shape for riding. Emily hitched up her skirt and climbed onto the fence beside the cow.

"I'm a circus horse rider!" she called as she grabbed hold of the cow's neck and flung one leg out over her back. Suddenly, the slow, calm cow transformed into a bucking, kicking wild creature. Emily tried to hold

on, but she lasted only a moment before she was thrown off into the mud beside the creek.

Alice and Lizzie screamed and ran to the cow yard fence.

"Milly! Are you hurt?" Alice cried.

Emily got slowly to her feet, rubbing her bruised backside. The cow had run off kicking to the other side of the yard. Now she was calmly chewing again, her tail switching lazily.

"It serves you right," Lizzie said. "You have such silly ideas, Emily. Imagine, pretending the cow was a horse. You couldn't ride a horse, anyway."

Emily scowled at Lizzie and turned back to the cow. It seemed that she wasn't good at anything. She walked over and stroked the cow's side.

"Sorry, cow," she whispered. "I won't try that again."

The cow looked at Emily with her soft eyes, her ordeal already forgotten. Sometimes animals were much nicer than people, Emily thought.

2
In Trouble Again

Emily hurried up the stairs into the kitchen at the back of the house. With all her strength, she pushed down on the handle of the pump at the kitchen sink. Water gushed out of the pump mouth and into the basin. She stopped pumping and scooped the cold water into her hands. Father would be home any minute, expecting to look over a row of clean, tidy children, and she was a mess.

Emily washed her hands and face quickly, and then raced from the room and up the stairs to the bedroom she shared with Alice and Lizzy. She didn't have time to change into a clean dress, but she tore off her soiled pinafore and pulled on a fresh one. Then she ran back down the stairs, buttoning the pinafore behind her as she went.

Dede stood at the bottom of the stairs, hands on her hips.

"For heaven's sake, Emily, slow down to a civilized pace and walk quietly. Mother is resting."

Emily slowed. She glanced up towards her mother's bedroom, which was upstairs at the front of the house. A faint cough made its way down to their ears, as if to emphasize Dede's words. Emily frowned. She hadn't wanted to disturb Mother. Sometimes she wished she could behave more like Dede and the others wanted her to. But it was hard always remembering to do this and do that and don't do this and don't do that.

Emily concentrated on walking quiet and ladylike out the front door to the garden. She took her place between Alice and their little brother, Richard, just as Father walked through the front gate.

Father strode up the walk between the rows of English flowers he'd planted.

Many were still blooming although winter was getting closer. He looked tall and important in his dark suit and hat. His eyes checked over the flowers. Then he seemed to notice the children for the first time, and he raised his walking cane slightly to greet them. He walked along the row of children, inspecting them like he had the flowers. Emily squirmed. Father stopped in front of her and frowned.

"That's not dirt I see on your face, is it, Emily?" he asked. He stepped closer and looked her over more carefully.

"There is dirt under your fingernails," he pointed out with disapproval. Then, he nodded downward. "And what is that?"

He bent closer. Emily pulled her hands behind her back. She'd forgotten about the drawing she'd done this morning on the back of one hand. She must have washed only the palms.

"Hands in front!" Father ordered, thumping his cane on the ground in front of Emily.

Slowly, Emily drew her hands out from behind her back.

"What is that?" he demanded.

"It's a face," Emily said, looking up past his tall black suit and square gray beard to meet his eyes. For a moment she thought she saw a twinkle of amusement there. Then Dede stepped up.

"I told her to stay clean," Dede said. "But all she does is misbehave. She should go without supper tonight."

"What!" exclaimed Emily. "All Dede does is boss, boss, boss. She should be the one to go without supper!"

"There!" Dede said. "That is the kind of insolence I have to put up with."

Father stamped his cane on the ground once more. His eyes had darkened like the sky suddenly covered by storm clouds.

"Emily, I won't have any more of that kind of talk. I am afraid you will have to go without supper while you work at improving your manners. You must show your sister more respect."

Emily looked down. Why couldn't anyone ever be on her side?

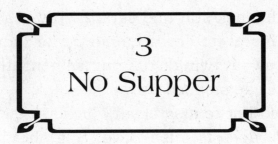

3
No Supper

At supper, Emily had to sit at the table with everyone else, but she was given nothing to eat. She stared down at the blank space in front of her, keeping her eyes from the food that seemed to cover every other spot, but it was hard not to breathe in the smell of roast beef and potatoes and not to listen to the sound of the others chewing. Little Richard, who sat beside Emily on her left, was an especially noisy eater. Worse, pieces of food kept falling from his fork onto her section of the table. Emily glanced up at Father and Dede. They seemed to be busy with their own food. Emily's hand crept onto the table.

"Emily!" Father barked.

Emily's hand froze, then retreated back to her lap, empty.

"You pick your food up, Richard," Mother said gently. She gave Emily a sympathetic look, and Emily sat on her hands, resolving to take her punishment more stoically for Mother's sake—even if she did feel it was unjust.

After supper, it was time for the children's weekly Saturday night bath. Dede dragged the big tub from the back porch into the middle of the kitchen and set pots of water boiling on the stove. When the tub was full, Lizzie shucked off her clothes and stepped into the steaming water. Dede helped to scrub Lizzie's back while Alice and Emily waited for their turns. Because she was the dirtiest, Emily went last.

By the time Emily climbed into the tub, the water had already cooled down. Dede dumped a fresh pot of boiled water around Emily's knees, nearly scalding her. Then, Dede set to work on Emily's back with the soap and scrub brush.

"Ouch!" Emily protested. She was sure Dede was scrubbing her skin much harder than she had Lizzie's or Alice's.

"Sit still, Emily," Dede ordered. "Remember, cleanliness is next to Godliness."

Emily clamped her teeth shut tight on the words that wanted to come out and worked at scrubbing the ink face off of her hand. She didn't want to give Dede any more opportunities to punish her tonight.

After the bath, Emily wrapped herself in a towel and ran up the stairs after her sisters. She put on a fresh nightgown and jumped into bed next to Alice. She pulled her knees up tight against her hungry stomach and wrapped her arms around them. She wished she had a puppy that would curl up next to her, warm and comforting. But Father had already told her he wouldn't allow a puppy. Puppies were hard to control. They made messes, had accidents on carpets, dug holes in flower gardens. Father kept his own dog, Carlow, chained up outside. But it would be so nice to have an animal of her own. A puppy would love her no matter what. A puppy wouldn't care if she got dirt under her fingernails or slid down banisters or sang too loudly or did things the way she wanted. Whatever that way was.

Emily wasn't sure what it was that she wanted to do or be. Alice wanted to grow up and be a mother. Lizzie wanted to be a missionary. It was easy for them. They were good at things. But Emily didn't seem to be good at anything—except, maybe, getting into trouble.

Emily's stomach growled. Tears stung the backs of her eyes. She felt as empty as her stomach.

Alice touched her shoulder, and Emily pretended to be asleep. Then she felt Alice's arm reach across her. Emily opened her eyes and saw that Alice was holding out something wrapped in a cloth napkin. The something smelled good.

"Thanks!" Emily whispered as she pulled the little bundle under the covers with her and sank her teeth into the delicious thick bread and cold meat.

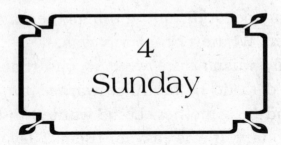

4
Sunday

"Rise up! Rise up! It's Sunday, children," Father called, stepping into the girls' bedroom.

Even if he hadn't said anything, Emily would have known it was Sunday by Father's smell—Wright's coal tar soap and camphor. Every Sunday Father washed with his special soap and dressed in clean clothes stored in the big camphor-wood chest of drawers, which he'd brought with him on a sailing ship from England.

Father left the room, and Emily climbed reluctantly out of bed. Some things she liked about Sundays and some things she didn't.

"Milly," Alice said, interrupting Emily's thoughts. She nodded meaningfully at the bed.

Emily took up her side of the bed covers and began straightening them. Once the bed was made Emily went to the wardrobe to take out her Sunday dress. Out of the corner of her eye she saw Alice lean over the bed to smooth out some wrinkles Emily had missed.

Emily pulled on her long black stockings, climbed into starched bloomers and petticoat, and wiggled her corset with its loosened laces down over her head. She adjusted the corset around her middle, then turned her back to Alice, sucked in her stomach and held her breath as Alice pulled the laces tight.

"Oh, I hate corsets!" Emily complained. "Why do I have to look like I have a tiny middle when I don't?"

"All ladies have to wear them," Alice said patiently, as she held in her own small stomach so that Lizzie could tighten and tie her corset laces. "Even young ladies like us."

"Well, I'd rather not!" said Emily.

Lizzie poked her head over Alice's shoulder and scowled at Emily.

"You'd rather be improper," scolded Lizzie.

As Lizzie turned back to the laces, Emily stuck out her tongue. Lizzie's eyes snapped back suspiciously, but Emily quickly pulled her stiff blue dress over her head, so that it hid her face. Once the dress was on, she had to turn to Alice again for help with all the tiny buttons she couldn't reach down her back. Finally, she buttoned on her tight black boots. Clothes were definitely one of the things she didn't like about Sundays.

Emily, Alice and Lizzie headed downstairs in their matching blue Sunday frocks. Emily's two oldest sisters, Dede and Tallie, said they were too old to dress the same, but Father insisted that at least his youngest daughters dress alike for church.

"I don't want my daughters looking like orphans," he'd say. "Only orphans have mismatched clothes."

Emily helped her sisters set the table in the dining room. That was the only work that could be done in the Carr house on a

Sunday. Sunday was the Lord's day of rest, which meant everyone else had to rest too and "think of God," as Dede said. Everything in the house was cleaned and polished extra well the day before, and all of Sunday's food was prepared on Saturday. The servant, Bong, milked the cow in the morning, then went away until evening milking time.

Once the table was set, it was time to leave for church. Mother was feeling better, but the two-mile walk to church would still be too difficult for her. Emily's second oldest sister, Tallie, and little Richard also found the walk hard, so they stayed home too. Everyone else set out for church, following Father across the back of the Carr property. The walk was one part of Sunday that Emily liked.

The air was cool and fresh. They followed a path through the cow's pasture, then came to a picket fence. Father lifted up a section of the fence that acted as a gate, and Emily's sisters stepped through. Emily came last, walking slowly. She didn't want to rush her favorite part of the walk. Ahead of her, tall pine trees stood amid grassy open spaces. In spring the grass would be full of wild lilies. Now, Emily stood, breathing in the memory of the flowers. She closed her eyes and saw them, dotting the ground in an unruly dance, their brown hearts bent close to the earth and their white petals reaching for the sky.

"Emily!" Dede called. "Hurry up or you'll make us late for church."

Emily sighed. She'd much rather stay here in the lily field—even without the lilies—than have to sit and listen to one of Dr. Reid's long sermons. But she followed Father and her sisters to the end of the field and out through another gate to the road.

The road was dry, so Emily, Alice and Lizzie held hands and walked down the middle of it. They only had to get out of the way of a horse and buggy once. This way was never busy—especially on Sundays. When the road was muddy they had to walk on the wooden sidewalk. Sometimes a cow, escaped from its pasture, stood on the sidewalk blocking their way. Dede would poke and wave her parasol, but it was never the cow that made way. Always it was Dede and the rest of them who had to step down into the mud and go around the cow. Emily was always secretly pleased when this happened, and she'd reach out to give the cow a friendly pat as she walked by.

As they neared the church, the sound of the church bell grew louder.

Bong. Bong. Bong.

They paused at the top of the hill outside the church and looked back the way they had come. Since Victoria had stopped being a Hudson's Bay Company fort and the fort walls had come down, the town had grown out farther and farther, swallowing more and more of the fields and forests around it. Only Beacon Hill Park still had some of its wildness. Emily could see the trees of the park just beyond her family's property, like the fur of a huge crouched animal looking out over the ocean. Closer to town near the bottom of the hill, the James Bay mud flats stunk with the smell of low tide. Dede wrinkled her nose as the smell wafted up to them, and she hurried everyone into church.

5
Following the Path

As Emily stepped inside the church, her eyes took a moment to adjust to the hazy light that shone down from the tall, pointed windows. She followed the others toward the front of the church and slid onto the hard bench seat next to Alice. Although the minister, Dr. Reid, had a loud voice, Father still liked to sit near the front, as he was going a little deaf, and he wanted to hear every word.

Emily was glad they had arrived early enough for her to watch the orphans file in and take their seats in the row ahead. None of them were dressed alike as Emily,

Alice and Lizzy were. The orphans wore clothes that other people had grown out of and donated to the orphanage, and some of the clothes were strange shapes and colors. The matron arranged the orphans so that the ones who were likely to misbehave sat between two who were well behaved, and the youngest ones sat in between older ones. Since the orphans sat in the front row, the stove was right in front of them.

Emily noticed Lizzy lean forward on the other side of Alice and bow her head. She guessed that Lizzy was probably thanking God that she was not an orphan.

When the church bell stopped ringing, a little door in front of the orphans opened, and Dr. Reid came out. He wore a black gown with two little white tabs in front that stuck out from under his beard like the tail of a bird. He carried a roll of paper in his hands, so that he looked like Moses holding the Ten Commandments. He walked slowly between the orphans and the stove and climbed up to the pulpit. The pulpit was wooden and rounded like the turret of a castle. Dr. Reid opened the Bible that sat on a red cushion on top of the pulpit. He leaned forward, and his deep voice boomed out over the rows of people.

Once he had got everyone's attention, Dr. Reid's voice settled into a fine deep rumble. The heat of the stove and the soothing sound of Dr. Reid's voice soon sent the orphans to sleep. The matron didn't seem to mind, since it kept them from whispering and fidgeting, and Dr. Reid was kind and did not bang the Bible or shout to wake them. Emily struggled to keep her own eyes open and to pay attention to Dr. Reid's words. She knew what would happen once they were home.

Finally, the sermon was over. Dr. Reid said his final "Amen," and the Carrs hurried home. They stopped only once to gather some catnip for Tibby, the cat. Dinner was waiting—cold mutton, red currant jelly, potato salad, pickled cabbage, bread and deep apple pie with Devonshire cream for dessert. When everyone had finished eating, Father folded his napkin straight and smooth. He looked down one side of the table and then the other. This was what Emily had been dreading. She tried not to squirm. If Father saw her squirm, he would pick her first.

"Emily." He'd seen her. "Tell me what you remember of the sermon."

Emily was silent. She'd tried to listen to Dr. Reid, and she hadn't fallen asleep this time, but the sermon had been so long and so dull. What had Dr. Reid said? All she could remember was something about sheep. She always liked the parts that talked about animals.

Emily swallowed and began, "God loved his people so much he sent Jesus to be a sheep."

Lizzie and Dede gasped.

"A sheep?" Father repeated, his mouth dropping open.

"Yes," Emily explained, uncertainly. "Dr. Reid said Jesus was the lamb of God."

Dede made a "humph" sound, and Father's face went red. Would Father ask Emily to say more? She wasn't sure what Dr. Reid

had meant; she'd just thought it sounded nice. She looked at Father. His face was still red, and if Emily hadn't known better she might have thought he was trying to hide a smile. He cleared his throat.

"And what do you remember?" he asked, moving on to Dede.

Emily relaxed. Her turn was over. Dede jumped here and there through the sermon, easily remembering each bit. When it was Lizzie's turn, she began at the beginning and plowed steadily through, repeating Dr. Reid's whole talk. Emily sighed. She would never be able to remember sermons as well as her sisters. She tried to pay attention, but her eyes kept moving to the window. Outside in the garden, spots of sunlight were dancing. Despite being stuck at the table, Emily felt something inside her give a little skip. She let her imagination sneak out the window and follow the beckoning light.

It wasn't until later in the afternoon, after Father had had his nap and Emily and her sisters had practiced their hymns and Bible verses, that Emily finally got out of the house for real. It was time for the Sunday walk around the Carr property. Father was ready with his black coat and yellow walking stick, and even Mother was downstairs and dressed with her hat on. Tallie was not strong enough for walking, so she lay on the sofa in the drawing room resting up for her evening visitor. Dede also stayed behind to play hymns on the piano and get the tea ready. Her booming piano chords followed Emily and the rest of the family out into the garden.

Father led the way out through a gate, then through another gate and out into the hawthorn shrubbery that ran around the cow yard. A small path ducked and twisted through the thorny bushes and was fun for games, but Father took the straight, clear path alongside the shrubbery. His walking stick poked and pushed at any branch, stick or rock that was out of place. Mother came behind him, holding little Richard's hand. Next came Alice, her arms hanging loose and floppy because she wasn't allowed to play with her dolls on Sunday. Next came Lizzie, her head held high and full of sermons. Emily came last, wishing their walk wasn't so fenced in by straight hedges and high wooden fences.

The sound of voices and laughter drifted from the road on the other side of the hedge. Emily parted the hedge with her hands and peaked through. Her friend Edna Green and her family were heading to the beach for their Sunday picnic.

"Hello, Edna," Emily whispered.

"Hello, Emily," said Edna, stopping. "Would you like to come to the beach with us?"

"I can't," Emily answered. She looked back towards Father. He didn't approve of picnics and fun on Sundays. He liked his family to stay home and walk with him.

"Too bad," said Edna. "Walking around your own cow field looks so dull."

"It is," Emily whispered back, hoping that none of her family heard.

Lizzie frowned at her when she ducked back through to the path.

For the rest of the walk, Emily was so busy wishing that she could go to the beach with the Greens that she almost missed the small yellow pansies poking up under the hedge. They must have grown from seeds on the wind. One stood right in the center of the path as if it didn't care what her Father or any of the others thought. Emily laughed to herself. One day she would do what she wanted too.

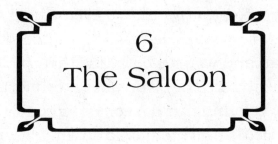

6
The Saloon

Early Monday morning Emily walked with her father along Carr Street as far as the James Bay Bridge. Father's store was over the bridge in the business section of town along Wharf Street. When Emily was smaller she sometimes went to work with Father, but now she said good-bye and turned to head to school. Under the bridge, the tide was on its way out. Emily saw a brown-skinned family, probably from the Songhees reserve, climbing into a canoe at the edge of the water. She paused, checked that Father was not looking back, and turned her attention to the man, woman and boy and their canoe. The boy hunched down in the middle of the canoe beside a small brown dog. Emily thought again of how she wished she had her own dog that would go everywhere with her. As the boat pulled away from the shore, the man and woman both dug their paddles into the water. They wore loose, comfortable looking clothing and seemed content and unhurried—as if they could do whatever they wanted and did not care what the corseted and stiff-suited townspeople thought.

Without thinking, Emily crossed the bridge, following the canoe. Even after it disappeared behind an anchored tall ship, she kept walking. What would it matter if she were a bit late for school? She needed a few minutes of freedom. Every morning, every day was the same. Father didn't like her to walk into town by herself, but she would just walk a bit further, then turn and run to school. Maybe she would get one glimpse of the outside of a saloon. Surely, that would be exciting. Dede and Father would never let her even look at a saloon. Whenever they passed one they'd pull her along and tell her to look straight ahead as if there were nothing to see. When she tried to get a glimpse past the swinging doors that the sailors and rough looking men passed through, a grown-up always blocked her view and yanked her ahead.

As she walked, nearing Fort Street, Emily heard a rumbling sound. At first she thought it might be thunder in the distance. She looked up, but the sky was blue and clear. As she turned onto Fort Street with its one-story offices and businesses close together, the rumbling grew louder. Suddenly, a huge cloud of dust full of terrible roaring and bellowing was coming right at Emily. She froze. Through the dust she could make out the shapes of cows. Hundreds of frightened, bellowing cows were thundering right up the middle of Fort Street, and she was right in their path. She was going to be trampled to death.

"Hey, there!"

Large, rough hands grabbed Emily and yanked her back from the road. The next instant she was in a large dim room looking out through swinging doors at the dust and cattle flowing past. The shouts of men and barks of dogs drifted in with the balling of the cows and the drumming of their hooves. A dust-covered man passed by the door, cracking a whip.

"Cattle drive," said a deep voice near Emily. "On their way to the slaughterhouse. Wouldn't do to get in their way."

Emily turned and looked into a broad dark face and a wide smile filled with gleaming white teeth. She smiled back shakily.

Slowly, Emily looked around her at tables, chairs and a long countertop with rows of shining bottles and glasses on shelves behind it. Behind them a long mirror reflected back the glasses and bottles so that it looked like there were twice as many of them. The legs of the wooden tables and chairs sank into a carpet of sawdust, and round shiny copper buckets sat on the floor by the tables and the counter.

"Welcome to the Beehive Saloon," said Emily's rescuer. He spat sideways, straight into one of the copper buckets. Spittoons, Emily realized.

Another man standing behind the bar counter poured some yellow liquid from a shiny silver tap into a glass and shoved it across the bar to Emily's rescuer. Taking the glass in one of his big hands, he threw back his head and gulped down the drink. Emily looked around her again. So this was what the inside of a saloon looked like.

Once the noise of the cattle had made its way up the street, Emily's rescuer held the swinging door open for her, and she headed back out into the still dusty street. She hurried away, coughing and disappointed. What had all the fuss been about? All that had been in the saloon were a few lonely dusty men and the smell of beer and sawdust. Emily hurried back over the bridge, dusting off her pinafore as she ran. At least it hadn't been a boring ordinary Monday.

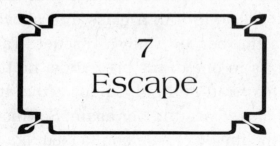

7
Escape

Out of breath, Emily arrived at Mrs. Fraser's house, where she attended school. Before Mrs. Fraser moved in, the little house had been called Marifield Cottage. Now it was referred to as Mrs. Fraser's school for young girls. Next year Emily would be walking the two miles to the public school with Alice and Lizzie, but for now she could still enjoy going to the little house in her own neighborhood. Mrs. Fraser's brother, Lennie, tended house while his sister taught school, and he let Emily in.

"You are late, Emily," Mrs. Fraser said with a frown when Emily appeared in the doorway of the room that had been made over into a classroom. The other girls looked up at Emily from the wide wooden desks that they shared, two to a desk.

Emily took a step toward the one empty seat, but Mrs. Fraser pointed past it to a stool at the back of the room—the dunce stool. This was where Mrs. Fraser sent anyone who misbehaved. Emily walked to the back of the room and climbed up onto the stool, smiling to herself. She didn't mind this punishment. Her trip to the saloon was worth it. Besides, the dunce stool was more comfortable than the regular desks. She knew this from past experience. You might even say the dunce stool was Emily's special seat.

The saloon visit remained Emily's secret. The days went back to being the same. The fall rains began, and each day Emily was scolded for the mud that ringed the bottom of her dress and pinafore. Then one weekend the sun came out again. Father was sick, and they had to walk to church on Sunday without him. On the way home, Emily looked with longing at the ocean beyond Beacon Hill Park. This was probably the last warm sunny day of the year, and she would be stuck at home.

When they arrived at the Carr house, Emily's friend Edna Green was waiting by the gate.

"Your mother said you could come with us today," Edna told Emily in an excited voice.

Could it be true? Emily glanced up to her father's bedroom window. Of course, there would be no family walk today with Father being sick. For once, he wouldn't miss her.

"I'll be right back!" Emily said, trying to keep her own excitement quiet—at least until she was safely away from the house. Then she ran inside to thank Mother and change her clothes. She pulled off her tight Sunday dress and corset and pulled on a loose frock and pinafore.

"Make sure you behave well," Mother told Emily. She said it with a smile as her hand reached out to Emily's face and tucked a stray piece of hair back into place. If it had been Dede, Emily would have scowled, but she smiled at Mother and nodded. She would try.

The beach was wonderful. The warm sun heated the cold wind that blew from the ocean. On the bluff above them stunted trees twisted away from the wind. Down below, Emily raced Edna and her two brothers along the gray sand. They clambered over logs, explored for shells and crabs and drew pictures in the sand with sticks. They played tag with the waves while the wind sang in their ears. Seagulls hung above them, screeching. Across the blue sky, huge clouds swirled like bold strokes of white paint. Emily climbed onto a rock and stood as tall as she could, her arms raised up over her head.

"Look at me!" she called, her voice rising up with the gulls.

"Dare you to walk out on that log," one of Edna's brothers called back, pointing to a log that had one end stuck between Emily's rock and another and the other end jutting out over the water.

"I double dare you!" challenged Edna's other brother.

"Don't do it, Emily," Edna cried from the sand beside her brothers.

Emily looked down at them from the rock. It was so wonderful to be out at the beach—to be wild and free like the waves and birds. She remembered her promise to Mother about behaving, but what could be wrong with walking on a log? Emily grinned down at her friends and stepped out. She walked slowly, balancing with her arms straight out to her sides. The wind whipped her dress and pinafore around her legs.

"You're such a show-off today," Edna teased, but she looked up at Emily with admiration.

Emily smiled and waved her arms dramatically. Then her foot slipped. The next thing Emily knew, she was sitting in the ocean — boots, stockings, dress and all.

That was it for the day at the beach. The Greens brought Emily home, dripping wet.

"How could you get into such a mess?" scolded Dede. "And on a Sunday of all days!"

Dede stomped toward the kitchen to heat water for a bath.

"Don't stand there dripping all over the hall," she called back over her shoulder. Shoulders slumped, Emily followed after her.

"Your sin will find you out," Lizzie whispered after them. She always had a Bible quote ready whenever Emily did something wrong. Emily glared back at Lizzie. She was glad Mother had gone upstairs to lie down.

That night Emily lay awake in bed, thinking about the day. She didn't feel sorry for having had such a good time, but she couldn't help feeling bad that she'd gotten everyone mad at her again. She tried to concentrate only on the wonderful things about the day—being near the ocean, running and laughing, feeling as free as the seagulls.

Finally, Emily fell asleep, dreaming about trying to balance on a log like on a seesaw—tipping one way and then the other. As hard as she tried, she couldn't seem to get it right.

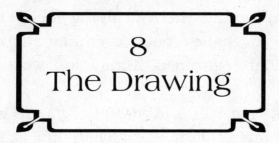

8
The Drawing

Emily found it hard to pay attention in school the next day. The memory of her day at the beach made the classroom seem even smaller and stuffier than usual. She dipped her pen in the inkwell and tried to do her work, but the letters on the page looked more like trees, waves or seagulls. The pen moved from her paper. She began to draw a smiling face on her hand—the face of someone at the beach. Smack! Mrs. Fraser's ruler hit the top of Emily's desk.

"Emily Carr! You will wash that mess off your hands and stay after school until you get your work right."

Much later, Emily walked home, dragging her feet on the dirt road. When she came to her house, she opened the gate and turned into the yard, then hesitated. She wasn't in a hurry to get inside and be scolded again. She headed towards the cow yard instead and stopped by Carlow's kennel. The old black dog was chained up beside his house. His tail thumped the ground as soon as he saw Emily. She knelt down beside him, and Carlow sniffed her face with his cool, wet nose. He was happy to see her no matter what. He didn't care if she had dirt on her pinafore and ink on her hands or if she behaved like a lady or not. She still wished she had a puppy of her own, but she always felt good when she was with Carlow. Dogs were even more comforting than cows or chickens.

Suddenly, Emily had an idea. She jumped up and ran into the house. She came back out carrying an old paper bag and a charred stick she'd found in one of the fireplace grates. She sat back down beside Carlow, tore open the bag and smoothed it out. Then she picked up the stick, looked at Carlow and began to draw.

Her eyes stroked his soft warm fur, while the charcoal stroked the paper. Emily forgot about everything else. When she was finished, she held up the drawing. Carlow looked back at her from the paper. Emily felt a warm glow inside her chest.

Later that evening, Emily showed her drawing, feeling anxious. She was sure she had done a good job, but would her family think so?

"It's very messy!" said Dede. "And you've got charcoal on your frock."

Father spread the drawing out on his desk and looked it over. He didn't say anything at first. At last he said, "Emily, I think you should have art lessons."

Emily waited for him to say more, but he didn't. She left the room, disappointed. She had wanted Father to tell her how good her drawing was and how much he liked it. But he hadn't. Or had he? Father had said she should have art lessons. Was that his way of telling her he thought she'd done well? Emily began to skip up the stairs. Art lessons! She was going to have art lessons!

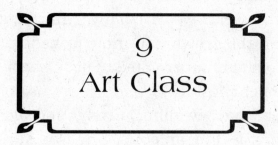

9
Art Class

The first art lesson was Monday after school.

Miss Woods, the art teacher, came to the school with a portfolio of pictures under her arm. These were prints, or copies, of real paintings and etchings, Miss Woods explained. A few looked like the illustrations Emily had seen in Father's *Sunday at Home* supplement, which sometimes featured fairy stories like *At the Back of the North Wind*. Occasionally Father would read one of these stories out loud to the family after reading the Bible on a Sunday evening. If there were illustrations, it was a special treat.

Miss Woods gave a picture and a piece of

paper to each student. She told everyone to try to copy his or her picture.

"We learn about art by studying the work of artists," the teacher explained. "We learn to draw by practicing drawing."

Emily looked at the picture in front of her, trying not to feel disappointed. The image was a bowl of fruit. She'd hoped at least for some trees or a horse grazing in a meadow, like the picture Miss Woods handed to the girl in the desk beside Emily. Still, Emily set to work eagerly. It wasn't nearly as thrilling as drawing Carlow, who had been alive and breathing right in front of her, but some of the joy she'd felt sketching the dog came back to her. It didn't matter what she drew, as long as she was drawing.

The next week Miss Woods brought in photographs for them to copy. Again, Emily set to work with enthusiasm.

"Don't press so hard on your pencil, Emily," Miss Woods instructcd as she walked by Emily's desk. When she got to the front of the room she stopped and smiled at her students.

"You are all doing very well, class," she said. "I can already see improvement from last week."

Had Miss Woods looked at Emily a little longer when she said this or had Emily merely imagined it? She wasn't sure, but she bent over her drawing again, feeling hopeful. Soon she was caught up in the feel of her pencil on the paper and the magic of the image taking shape under her fingers. It didn't matter what the teacher or anyone else thought. Emily loved art lessons. Finally, she had found something she liked to do, and she wanted to learn everything she could about it. The more she learned, the more excited she grew about art.

It wasn't until her drawings were finished and the feeling of magic had seeped away, that Emily worried about whether they were any good. When she looked around at the other girls' artwork doubt crept through her. She wasn't good at anything else, so how could she be good at art? She pushed the worry away and let her new love of art take over.

At home, Emily practiced drawing whenever she could. She even made an easel out of branches that Father had pruned from the old cherry tree outside her bedroom window. She took three of the straightest branches, tied them together at the top, spread them out at the bottom, and put two nails in the wood to hold a drawing board. She placed the easel in front of the dormer window in her bedroom and propped a piece of paper on the drawing board. She was beginning to feel like a real artist.

"I wish you wouldn't spend so much time drawing," Alice grumbled as she swept the floor around the legs of the easel.

"But I have to practice if I want to be an artist," Emily said.

"An artist?" Alice said. "Ladies don't become artists. It's good to be accomplished in drawing and painting, as well as things like embroidery and music, but you'll have no time to be an artist when you're a wife and a mother."

"Then I won't be a wife and a mother," Emily said.

Alice looked shocked for a moment, then she smiled and shook her head. She went back to sweeping, and Emily knew Alice was thinking that Emily was being silly again and would change her mind soon enough.

I won't change my mind, Emily said to herself. But could she do it? Could she be a real artist? Doubt crept back into her, niggling at her like an itch. She tried to put Alice's words about ladies not being artists out of her mind.

10
Dede's Visitors

Emily continued to go to art lessons and to practice drawing at home. She even found an old set of watercolor paints and some old brushes and was thrilled when color appeared on her paper. Still, her work seemed to be nothing more than sketches with color. She still had a lot to learn.

In class, Miss Woods told them that to be a real artist you had to go to art school. At art school the students drew from statues and plaster casts, and sometimes they sketched live models. Emily saved her pocket money and bought plaster casts of hands, lips, noses and eyes from the Victoria tombstone maker who used the casts to help him model angels for his tombstones.

At home, Emily set the plaster casts on the windowsill in front of her easel where she could look at them and draw. She filled paper after paper with hands, lips, noses and eyes. She felt satisfied with her work, but still, she felt that itch of uncertainty. Were the drawings any good? She couldn't tell.

One day, Emily stood at the window in her bedroom looking out at the bare branches of trees and the gray sky. She felt restless. Suddenly, Emily wanted to be outside. She set down her paintbrush and hurried out of the room to the top of the stairs. She paused, looking down over the glossy wood railing. No one was around. Surely no one would notice if she took one slide down the banister.

"Wait!" Alice called from behind her. She hurried after Emily.

"Dede has guests in the drawing room," she warned Emily in a whisper. "It's Mr. and Mrs. Smith, the artists."

"They're both artists?" Emily asked. She leaned farther over the railing, straining to catch a glimpse of the guests through the drawing room door at the bottom of the stairs.

"Yes," Alice answered. "That's what Dede said. They're visiting from England. Please don't lean so far out, Milly."

For Alice's sake, Emily stopped leaning. She couldn't see anything, anyway.

"But I thought you said ladies couldn't be artists?" Emily said.

"Well, the Smiths have no children, and perhaps Mrs. Smith is wealthy enough to do as she wishes," Alice suggested.

Emily wasn't listening. Whatever the reason, a real artist was a real artist. She wanted to get a closer look. Step by step, she tiptoed down the stairs. Maybe they would talk about art. Maybe she could pick up some clues that would help her become a real artist.

Voices drifted up to her from the drawing room. One was Dede's voice, politely inquiring. A male voice with an English accent answered. Emily got to the bottom of the steps and crept to the side of the drawing room door.

"How are you enjoying sketching our Canadian landscape?" Dede's voice asked.

"I'm afraid it is too wild for my taste," drawled the man's voice. Emily bristled. Too wild? What did he mean? She loved the forests and ocean around Victoria. How could anyone think they weren't beautiful?

"Why, yes," a high pitched woman's voice added. "In England and France the elements in a landscape arrange themselves into a composition. Here, nature is so vast and unruly, one does not know where to look."

"I do know what you mean," said Dede's careful voice. "Wildness is one of the drawbacks of living in the colonies, but I do think we have done very well with what we have here."

"Indeed," the man's voice agreed, though he sounded unconvinced.

Emily could stand it no longer. She leapt into the doorway, her fists balled at her sides, her face red with outrage.

"Snobs!" The word burst from her. "If you can't see what is in front of you, you're both blind!"

"Emily!" Dede's face was dark with shock and anger. "That is enough."

Emily clamped her mouth shut. Suddenly, she felt shocked herself. She hadn't meant to burst in. She hadn't meant to say anything. She stared into the faces of Dede's well-dressed guests. The man leaned back in his chair, his hand holding a teacup, frozen on its way to his mouth. His face had a twisted look as if he couldn't decide whether he should be angry or amused. The woman's eyes had narrowed from surprise to disapproval.

"Emily, you must apologize to our guests at once!" Dede said.

Emily was silent.

"Emily," Dede repeated. Emily heard the cold warning in her voice.

Emily looked down at the floor. "I am sorry for speaking rudely to you," she said. Then she added, "And I'm sorry for you."

"Sorry for us?" asked the man with a laugh.

Emily wanted to say she was sorry that they were such stupid snobs, but Dede glared at her. "I mean only that I am sorry you can't appreciate the beauty of Canada," she said.

The man made a "humph" sound, and the woman looked shocked again. Dede darkened even further.

"You must excuse me for a moment," she said to her guests as she got up from her seat and marched toward Emily. She took hold of Emily's elbow, pinching tightly, and led her from the room. Emily knew she was in trouble now. But she didn't care. What horrible people! If that's what real artists were like, how could she ever be one?

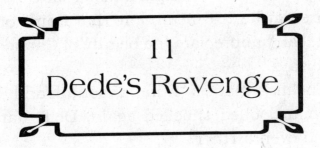

11
Dede's Revenge

When Dede told Father about Emily's rudeness, he decided she should go without supper again. If she missed many more suppers she would not need the corset to have a tiny middle, Emily thought to herself. Still, she did not regret her words to the horrible artists. If they were what art was about, she didn't want to have anything to do with it.

Several days later, Emily was still smoldering from the memory of the snobby artists. Dede noticed her dark looks.

"For heaven's sake, Emily. You aren't still mad about the Smiths, are you?" Dede asked, her hands on her hips.

"They didn't know what they were talking about," Emily complained.

"Oh, they didn't, did they?" Dede's face set into firm lines of decision. "You wait until Saturday, and you will see."

Emily wondered what Dede could mean. The look on Dede's face made Emily feel a sense of dread as she waited for the weekend to come.

"I'm taking Mrs. Lewis for a drive," Dede announced Saturday morning. Dede was always visiting elderly or invalid people like old Mrs. Lewis. Often, in warmer weather, she hooked up the horse and buggy and took them for drives along country roads, but Emily wasn't sure where Dede would be taking Mrs. Lewis on a cold November day.

"And Emily is coming too," Dede added.

Emily's insides felt suddenly heavy. She had been hoping that Dede had forgotten about her and whatever she'd said would happen on Saturday. Now what? Perhaps Dede was planning to bore Emily to death, as a long ride with old Mrs. Lewis and her many ailments was sure to do.

Dede packed an extra warm blanket in the buggy to put over Mrs. Lewis's legs, and they were off. They drove along Carr Road, which was named after Father because he had donated a strip at the front of his property for the widening of the road. The road became Government Street at the James Bay Bridge. It was still narrow, but wider than the meandering cart trail it had once been. Many of the roads in Victoria had started off as trails or cow paths.

When they reached Mrs. Lewis's house, Dede helped the old woman into the buggy and bundled blankets around her.

"This is so kind of you, Miss Carr," said Mrs. Lewis, her round wrinkled face pink with excitement. "I haven't been to an exhibition in years."

An exhibition of what, Emily wondered.

"It's not really an exhibition," said Dede. "It's just a few pieces of art on display at the home of the Bellevilles."

"Of course," said Mrs. Lewis. "But it's more than I've enjoyed since I was last in England."

Emily squirmed with excitement. Was Dede actually taking her to see an exhibition of art? There were a few dusty old portraits and naval scenes in some of the homes Emily had visited, but these were the only paintings Emily had seen. Surely an exhibition of real art would be more exciting—wonderful even.

Dede drove the buggy through town and stopped in front of a large new house. She helped Mrs. Lewis up the wide front stairs and knocked on the door. A servant girl let them in.

"Miss Carr, Mrs. Lewis, I'm so glad you could come," said the tall, well-dressed woman who appeared behind the servant, holding her hands out to them. "And this must be young Emily."

"Good afternoon, Mrs. Belleville," Dede said, smiling at the woman. Then she turned to Emily and gave her a warning look. "Behave!" that look said.

"Please, come into the drawing room," the woman said, directing them with a graceful wave of one hand. "The Smiths have been so gracious in allowing me to display some of their paintings."

Emily's mouth dropped open. The Smiths? She glowered at Dede. How could Dede let Emily get so excited and then give her the Smiths? Her first art exhibition, and it was already ruined. How could she possibly enjoy the paintings now?

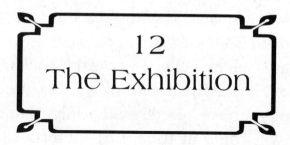

12
The Exhibition

Dede saw Emily's sour face and gave her a pinch. Feet dragging, Emily followed the ladies into the drawing room. At least the Smiths themselves weren't here, she told herself. Perhaps their paintings would be nicer than they were.

The Bellevilles' drawing room was larger and fancier than the Carrs'. Mrs. Belleville pointed out the many pieces of furniture that had come all the way from England.

"Please sit," she said, helping Mrs. Lewis over to a large chair of polished wood and embroidered cushions.

"Of course," she added, waving a hand at several paintings displayed on the walls around them, "this is nothing like the real exhibitions of art Mr. Belleville and I attended when we were last in London. Our good friends in England were appalled to hear that Victoria has no galleries or artist societies."

"Yes, such organizations are luxuries we do not yet have," Dede said stiffly. "I'm sure they will come in time, but Victoria is still so new. There is more important work to attend to first—such as the creation of a women's Christian society."

Emily scowled and turned her back on the women. If they'd come to look at the paintings, why weren't they looking at them? She walked over to a small watercolor. She was determined not to like anything created by the Smiths, but her eyes roved hungrily over the painting. It was a soft delicate scene of a lake surrounded by trees. She had to admit the picture was pretty. She liked the feeling of sunlight on the green leaves. But the arrangement of lake and trees seemed too perfect to Emily. She remembered Mrs. Smith's high voice saying how the landscape in England and

France arranged itself into a composition so much better than the unruly wild scenery of British Columbia. The Smiths seemed to imply that only well-behaved landscapes could be painted, and that British Columbia was much too wild and disordered to interest any real artist. Emily bristled as she moved to the next painting.

Mrs. Belleville noticed her.

"That one was painted right here in British Columbia," Mrs. Belleville said with pride.

The painting Emily was now looking at showed faraway mountains partly hidden behind thin wispy mist. In the foreground, a small house had been given a curved roof like an Eastern temple. It didn't look like any of the houses Emily had ever seen, and the mountains and mist didn't look familiar either. Nothing about the picture looked like it had been painted in Canada.

"The Smiths are such fine artists," Mrs. Belleville was saying. "Victoria is lucky to have them compliment us with a visit."

Emily turned away to hide her disgust. The Smiths' visit a compliment to Victoria?

Ha! The woman had obviously not heard the Smiths talk, and she hadn't noticed that they hadn't tried to paint what they saw here either. All they had painted were romantic imaginary landscapes.

An angry remark rose in Emily's throat, but she swallowed it. She might not like the Smiths or their impressions of Canada, but they did seem to know how to paint, and Emily didn't want to be sent out to sit in the buggy before she finished looking at all the paintings.

13
The Praying Chair

"There!" Dede said once she and Emily had returned home. "Now that you have seen real art perhaps you will keep your mouth shut about matters you know nothing about."

Emily didn't say a word. Her mind was full of confusing thoughts. She seethed at the Smiths' snobbery, and their paintings had been disappointing, but Dede was right. The Smiths were real artists, and Emily wasn't. She would never be able to paint like they could. She didn't want to, she told herself. She wasn't interested in their phony, well-behaved landscapes. Despite all of this, seeing real paintings stirred something inside Emily—something that made her want to race up the stairs to her easel, pick up her pencils and brushes and create something of her own.

She made herself climb slowly up the stairs to her room and not look at the easel that stood by the window. How simple and joyful it had been to do the sketch of Carlow, and how happy she had been to have art lessons. She wished she hadn't heard of the Smiths and their snobby painting ideas. Now she didn't know what to think. She imagined Carlow out in his kennel—his warm fur and comforting licks. At least there was nothing to be confused about where dogs were concerned. Sometimes it seemed they were the only things in her life Emily was sure about. No matter what, she still wanted a dog.

Emily had always wanted a dog of her own—a soft chubby puppy that would wag its tail and come to her whenever she called. It was almost December now. Her birthday was coming, and it had been a long time since Emily had last asked Father if she could have a puppy.

Emily put art out of her mind, and thought more and more about her birthday. On the first day of December she climbed out of bed into the chilly air and pulled out the basin of water that was kept under the bed. She dipped her hands in the icy water and splashed some onto her face. Father believed that children should wash with cold water every morning. If Emily skipped a morning wash, Father was sure to ask her about it.

Before breakfast the family gathered in the sitting room for their morning prayer. Father sat in his new wicker chair and reached for the small book of prayers that sat on the round table beside him. The others knelt on the floor in front of their own chairs while Father read the prayers. Emily liked to kneel in the bay window and bury her face in the windowseat cushion, but today Father asked her to kneel beside him. Emily knelt and ducked her head under one arm of the wicker chair. She'd much rather be by the window where she could sneak a peek outside now and again. Instead, she snuck a look at Tibby, the cat, who was curled up behind Father's chair close to the warmth of the fireplace. Tibby was the only one who looked comfortable.

As Father prayed, the chair creaked and whispered as if it were trying to pray too.

Emily whispered a silent prayer of her own. "Please let me have a puppy. I don't care about its size or shape or color—just as long as it's a real live dog."

When Father finally finished reading and leaned forward to reach for his bookmark, the chair squawked an "Amen" as grand as Father's. Tibby joined in with a loud meow. Emily smiled to herself. God had heard her prayer for sure.

"Oh dear," said Mother, rising to her feet. "Father's chair has pinched Tibby's tail. Take her outside, Emily."

14
The Birthday Present

As the thirteenth of December, Emily's eighth birthday, approached, Emily's hope for a puppy grew.

"I know something is coming for your birthday," Dede told her in one of her better moods.

"Is it...?"

"Wait and see," Dede said.

Emily wiggled with excitement. How could she wait? She needed to know—even just a hint.

"Does it start with a 'd' or maybe with a 'p'?" she askcd.

"I think it does," Dede said with a smile.

The day before Emily's birthday she couldn't help singing more loudly than usual as she did her chores after school. She brought the chickens their food and checked for eggs in the hen house. She sang out greetings to the cow who stood near the barn waiting for Bong to come to her for the afternoon milking.

Dede appeared on the back porch.

"Hush, Emily," she scolded. "That noise of yours will scare the neighbors!"

Emily took her excitement away from the house and out to the woodshed. She dug out a wooden box and dusted it off, hoping it would be the right size for her puppy. Then she went to the garbage pile where discarded items waited for the spring bonfire. She poked around until she found an old brush that Alice had thrown away a month ago. It still had a few bristles left and would do for a dog brush.

Emily carried her supplies back to the house. She waited until no one was around, then quickly smuggled them up to her bedroom and hid them under her bed. She found a knitted blanket that belonged to an old worn doll and placed it in the box under the bed. Then she braided a collar out of blue and green cord and sewed on some hooks and eyes at varying distances, since she wasn't sure how big the dog would be. Now she was ready.

The morning of Emily's birthday arrived. Morning prayers seemed to take forever. "Hurry! Hurry!" Emily wanted to call out. "I want to see my puppy!" Finally, Father's chair squeaked its concluding "Amen!" Everyone took turns giving Emily a birthday kiss, and they all filed into the breakfast room. Emily hurried ahead, anxious and excited.

There on her plate was a flat flat parcel.

"Open it!" Lizzie and Alice urged her.

Emily looked around the room, but there was no other present. She began to untie the string of the flat parcel, her hands shaking.

"I'm glad to see, Emily, that you remembered your morning wash even on your birthday," Father said, noticing Emily's hands.

Emily tried to smile, but her hands were not trembling from cold. The happy feeling

she'd woken with this morning had drained away. As the parcel wrapping fell to the floor, Emily tried not to cry.

The present was a framed picture of a little girl holding a dog in her arms. It was a pale and tiny copy of a painting like one of Miss Woods' prints—lifeless.

"She looks like you," Alice pointed out.

"No, she isn't like me," Emily said in a hard voice. "She has a dog."

Emily went to the fireplace at the end of the room, pretending to warm her hands. She slipped the blue and green collar from her pinafore pocket and dropped it into the fire.

"I'm not hungry," she said. "I'm going out to feed the chickens."

That day took a long time to end. In the afternoon, Mother came and felt Emily's forehead and asked her if she was feeling sick. Emily shook her head and tried to smile for Mother.

Emily climbed into bed that night without saying her prayers. What good was it to pray for anything? What good was it to wish?

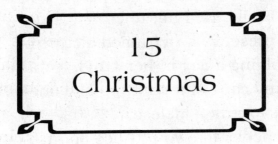

15
Christmas

Although Emily had tried to put art out of her mind, she found that drawing helped to ease her disappointment about her birthday. When she stood at her easel, her pencil or paintbrush at work, she forgot about everything except the joy of what she was doing. She decided that it would be much better to keep the Smiths and what they stood for out of her mind, than to keep art out. She dove back into her drawing practice, filling more pages with noses, hands, feet and faces. As Christmas drew closer, she became further distracted by the preparations and growing excitement.

The day before Christmas, the Carr house

filled with the spicy smell of boiling plum pudding and the fresh fir scent of the Christmas tree. On Christmas Eve Father took Emily and her younger sisters into town to see the shops lit up. Every lamp-post had a fir tree tied to it, and the shop windows were decorated with mock snow made of cotton wool and sparkly dust. In the grocer's window was a Santa Claus grinding coffee. Bonbons, clusters of raisins, nuts, candied fruits and long peppermint candy sticks surrounded him. At the end of the food shops was Chinatown. Its dark streets held no Christmas decorations. Emily's father turned them around to head back to James Bay.

Before bed the children hung their stockings from the high mantelpiece in the breakfast room, and Dede read "'Twas the Night before Christmas and all through the house, not a creature was stirring, not even a mouse..."

At the bottom of the stairs Emily peeked into the dark dining room and smelled the Christmas tree waiting there. She couldn't see it, but she knew that it stood there, touching the ceiling and hanging heavy with presents ready for the morning. Up in her bedroom the air was chilly, and Emily dove under the covers next to Alice. She wiggled with excitement.

"Be still," whispered Alice. "I want to sleep."

Emily tried to keep still, but she tossed one way and then the other. How could she fall asleep when there were presents waiting? She tried not to think of the new set of paints she wanted or of the cuddly puppy she had longed for. She knew it wouldn't do any good to wish for them, but she couldn't help hoping that something special hung on the tree for her.

Morning finally came, and they were off to church. After church, Father went into the dining room to light the candles on the Christmas tree. Then he called everyone in, and they held hands around the tree to sing Christmas carols. Then, one by one, the presents were taken down from the tree and handed out. Emily held her breath as she unwrapped each of her presents. Everything was practical, as usual: gloves from Dede, embroidered hankies from Alice and Lizzie, new black boots from Mother. No puppy. No art supplies.

I don't care, Emily told herself. I'll never be good enough to be a real artist, anyway.

16
Mill Stream

Winter seemed to last a long time, but finally the green buds of new leaves appeared on the trees outside Emily's window. Father was in a good mood and promised the family a picnic the following Saturday. The days before the picnic crawled along. The hands of the clock seemed to stick in one place and Emily thought Saturday would never come. But it did.

Emily's aunt and uncle were visiting from San Francisco, so Father ordered the omnibus to pick them up and take them out to Mill Stream. The bus was yellow with carpeted seats. Emily's uncle made a nest of cushions in one corner for Aunty.

The baskets of food were tucked in around her, then the children climbed in. Emily settled on one of the high seats. Up ahead, the driver called for the two horses to be off. The bus jerked and rattled over the dirt roads. The wheels were rimmed with iron and made a terrible clanging sound over the stones. Emily's body swayed, and her dangling legs bumped against the bottom of the seat. She began to feel queasy. She climbed up onto her knees and rested her arms on the open window ledge. That was better.

On her nest of cushions Aunty coughed and held a white lace handkerchief up to her face.

"The dust is going to ruin my new coat," she complained. She waved her hankie at Uncle, and he hurried to close Emily's window. Emily went back to bumping and swaying and feeling queasy.

Finally, the omnibus came to a stop. The driver opened the door and everyone spilled out onto a grassy clearing beside a stream. Emily stood, drinking in the sight of meadow and forest, the smell of new green, the tinkling sound of the moving water. Behind her, Lizzie pushed past, carrying a basket. Reluctantly, Emily turned back to help unload the bus.

Soon, Dede had a tablecloth spread across the grass, and she and Mother were removing cloth bundles from the baskets and unwrapping cakes, pies, cold meat and sandwiches. Uncle made a new nest of cushions for Aunty next to the table-cloth.

"Lunch first, children," said Mother. "Then you can play."

After they hurried through their food, Emily, Alice and Lizzie jumped to their feet and headed to the stream. Little Richard followed them.

"Keep by the stream," Mother called after them. "Don't go into the woods—and watch out for your brother."

"You have four hours," Father called, holding up his watch on its chain.

Emily sighed happily. Four hours was a wonderfully long time. She walked slowly, poking along the edge of the stream. They followed it into the forest, though they stayed close to the water as Mother had directed. The woods were too thick to get into, anyway. Pine and cedar trees towered overhead, smelling spicy and sweet. The stream made a tunnel through the dark, shadowy forest. This was the type of wild place Emily loved.

She climbed from rock to rock. In one spot the stream rushed around a huge boulder and bubbled into a pool. In another spot the stream was gentle and slow. Mossy stones looked like babies' heads, which Alice pretended to be giving a bath. Many-fingered ferns hung over the banks, dipping into the water. Around a bend, there was a muddy beach with mysterious heart shaped prints.

"Deer hooves," said Lizzie.

Emily imagined the gentle deer coming to the stream to drink. She sat down on her knees and bent forward. In front of her the water looked clear and fresh. She was thirsty.

"Milly!" Alice cried in alarm, catching hold of the back of Emily's pinafore as she began to topple over into the stream.

Emily flung out her hands to help stop her fall. One of them went into the stream, but her sleeve was only wet up to the elbow. Not too bad, Emily thought.

Plop! Something jumped into the water beside Emily.

Splash! Both Emily's sleeves went in up to the elbows this time. She pulled her hands out of the water, triumphantly holding a large, golden-brown toad.

"Ugh!" said Lizzie and Alice together. "You'll get warts."

Emily turned her back on them and held the toad for little Richard to see. His eyes opened wide as he stared at the toad. He smiled in appreciation. Emily put the toad in a tin and placed a large skunk cabbage leaf over top for a lid, then she hid it under a plant to collect later.

Suddenly, Dede appeared from around the bend behind them.

"It's time to go home," she said.

"It is not!" Emily cried. They'd hardly been gone long at all.

Dede gave Emily an angry pinch, then turned to take little Richard's hand. For the first time, Emily noticed that he looked tired.

"It's been four hours," Dede said as she began to march them back.

Emily hung behind to pick up the toad. She looked up into the silent trees. Only the stream made any sound. How could a few hours have gone so quickly when Saturday had taken so long to arrive?

She said good-bye to the forest and stream and followed the others back. At the picnic site, the baskets were already packed, and Uncle was building a new nest for Aunty in the omnibus. Mother was seated in the bus, looking tired. Richard climbed up beside her and laid his head on her lap. He was instantly asleep. His toy watch dangled out of his pocket. The hands had not moved since they'd started on the trip that morning. The toy watch is much truer than Father's real one, Emily thought.

She sat down across from Aunty. The bus rolled and bumped along. Emily peeked under the skunk cabbage leaf she'd placed over the toad's tin.

"Emily dear," said Aunty in an indulgent voice. "You must throw that leaf out of the window. The smell is upsetting your old aunty."

Reluctantly, Emily tossed the leaf out the window.

"What do you have in the tin, dear?" asked Aunty.

Annoyed that Aunty had made her throw out the leaf, Emily thrust the tin up to the old woman's face.

Aunty screeched.

Dede reached across, took the tin and looked inside. Before Emily could stop her, she flung it out the window, toad and all.

Emily swallowed a cry and twisted around to look. As the omnibus clattered forward, the tin can bounced off into the bushes at the side of the road. She could just make out the golden-brown shape of the toad hopping slowly back toward the stream.

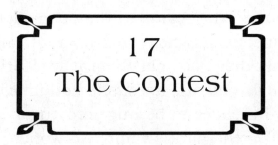

17
The Contest

Sitting in the hard, wooden desk at school the next week, Emily couldn't stop her mind from wandering back to the stream. She wondered how the toad was doing. Only art class could keep her attention. In other classes, the time dragged, but in art class it flew just as it had at the stream. She had tried to stop being interested in art, but it was something inside her that had taken hold. She couldn't shake it off.

Art was like the British Columbia nightingales. This was a nickname Father had given to the tree frogs that sang each spring in Beacon Hill Park. It was hard to believe that such a tiny creature could make such a big noise. When she was smaller Emily had been frightened by the chirping rattling sound that came in the open window and filled the whole bedroom at night. When Father had told them it was British Columbia's nightingales, she had imagined the nightingales to be huge creatures lying in wait in the park swamp. No wonder her parents had forbidden her to wander alone through the park.

Then Mother had told Emily that a nightingale was an English bird that didn't live in Victoria at all and that the name was just Father's idea of a joke. Now Emily loved the sound of the frogs in spring. All winter you heard nothing from them, then suddenly they were there, filling the whole world with their sound. Art was like that inside Emily. Now that it had woken, she couldn't keep it quiet. She was like the frogs too — not a beautiful English singing bird, but a spunky creaking British Columbia frog. And she liked it.

At home she continued to draw at her easel, and Alice continued to complain about

86

sweeping around the legs. Sometimes it seemed to Emily, though, that the complaining was just habit, and Alice didn't really mind. Once, Alice had even told her that she thought Emily's drawing was improving, but Emily was sure she'd only said it to be nice. Lizzie had not said anything nice when she tripped over one of Emily's large plaster noses. She still thought Emily was wasting her time with art. Emily scowled at Lizzie and tried to ignore her words, but she felt discouraged. With all her heart, Emily wished she could be an artist. But wishes had disappointed her too many times.

One art class, Miss Woods announced that they were going to have a contest to see who could copy the best.

"Once you have learned how to copy," explained Miss Woods, "you can begin drawing from life."

The idea of drawing from life was exciting. Copying pictures was getting dull. Miss woods gave Emily a picture of a boy holding a rabbit. Emily looked at the picture. She tried to imagine drawing a real live rabbit, and thought about what the rabbit would feel like in her own arms. She remembered the day she drew the picture of Carlow—his warm fur and his wet nose. The rabbit's nose would twitch. Its fur would be softer. Emily's pencil moved across the paper. She forgot about the other children. The lines of the pencil and the imagined feel of the rabbit blended together and filled Emily.

When she was finished, Emily put down her pencil. She felt light and happy.

Miss Woods walked around the room, looking carefully at each of the children's drawings. She held up one that a girl named Bessie Nuthall had done. The picture of a girl with a basket was very neat and carefully drawn. The winner for sure, Emily thought. But then Miss Woods put the drawing down and walked on. She picked up Emily's. She seemed to be frowning at the smudged lines, and Emily sank down in her seat. Her happy feeling seeped away. It was hopeless. She would never be good at anything.

"This is the winner!" Miss Woods announced with a big smile.

It was Emily's picture.

"It's not the neatest," said Miss Woods. "But it's got the most life in it."

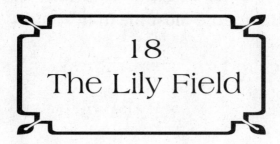

18
The Lily Field

When Emily walked home from school she felt so light her feet barely touched the ground. The road was muddy from spring rain, so she ran along the wooden sidewalk and jumped off at the gate in front of the Carr house. First, she went to Carlow's kennel and crouched down to pet him. His muddy paws left marks on her pinafore, but she didn't care. His tail wagged happily, and Emily felt that if she had a tail it would be wagging too. Then, she ran into the house.

Dede was just coming out of the kitchen.

"Quiet!" she snapped. "Mother is resting."

Emily stopped as suddenly as if she'd

bumped into a wall. Dede was never happy with anything she did. She probably wouldn't like Emily's new drawing. She'd think it was messy like the Carlow drawing. She probably wouldn't care about the contest. Slowly, Emily held out her picture.

"Look," she whispered. "My drawing was picked the best in the whole class."

"It's not nice to be boastful," Dede scolded. But she took the drawing and looked at it.

"You won a contest?" she asked. Did her voice soften? Were the corners of her mouth turning up? Emily wasn't sure.

"Yes," Emily said.

"Well, well," Dede said. "Very good."

Had Dede actually said "very good"? Emily wanted to leap into the air. She, Emily, had done something good. But Dede's voice stiffened again, and her face went back to being stern.

"If you'd try to be less messy, you'd do better," she added.

"Yes, Dede," Emily answered. For once, she didn't care about Dede's scolding. She held tight to the important words, "very good."

Emily hurried up the stairs to her room. She propped her picture up on the cherry branch easel. Then she went back out to the landing. First, she leaned over and checked to see if Dede was gone from the hallway and no one else was there. Then, she lifted up her skirt, flung one leg over the banister and slid down to the bottom of the stairs. She skipped out of the house, careful not to bang the door.

For once, no one called after her. No voice scolded, "Be good, Emily. Behave, Emily."

Emily walked to the cow yard, singing out hello to the cow, the rooster and the chickens. But she didn't climb the fence and go in. Instead, she walked past the cow pasture and on to the picket fence that surrounded the lily field. She didn't try to lift the picket gate. She just climbed over.

This time she did not have to imagine the lilies as she had during the winter. They were in full bloom. Emily stood in the middle of the delicate white flowers and looked up to the sky with them.

"I'm going to be an artist," she said out loud.

She had won a contest today, and even Dede had said she'd done well. Maybe it was just a little contest, and maybe her picture had been a bit smudgy, but it was a start. It meant she could be good at something, something that she, Emily, wanted to do. And she could do what she wanted. She could be an artist. She would keep telling herself that—no matter what other people said.

Emily drank in the perfume of the lilies and looked up through the tall pine trees. She felt that same strange, wonderful feeling she always felt in this spot. It filled her up and overflowed. She felt like she could float on her happiness right up over the lily field and fly like the wind out over the wild forest of Beacon Hill Park and the ocean beyond.

Afterword

Emily Carr was born in Victoria, British Columbia in 1871. She grew up at a time when people expected girls and women to behave only in certain ways. Emily didn't always fit people's expectations—when she was a girl or when she was grown up. Instead, she learned to follow her heart and believe in herself (even though it wasn't always easy). She studied art in San Francisco, England and France. Eventually, she began painting the wild places of the British Columbia west coast that she loved so much.

Even Emily's paintings were not what people expected. Instead of painting all the details of a landscape with tiny careful brush strokes, she used color, movement, light and space to show the feeling of life in the places she visited. She also painted things people had not seen painted before. She traveled all along the British Columbia coast, sketching and painting First Nations villages and wild places.

Emily continued to love animals, but she didn't get a dog of her own until she was grown up. After that, she always had lots of animals around her, including birds, dogs and even a monkey.

When Emily's health began to fail and she could no longer paint as much as she wanted to, she began to write. Even people who didn't understand or like her paintings liked the books she wrote about her life. If she were still alive today, Emily Carr would be pleased and surprised to know she is one of Canada's most famous and well-loved artists.

Emily's father did not live to see her become a real artist and to tell her she'd done well. But years after his death, Emily found the old drawing of Carlow saved in a drawer in his desk. He really had liked it, and he had been proud of her even then.

Jacqueline Pearce is the author of several books for children and teens, including *The Reunion* (Orca, 2002). She lives in Burnaby, British Columbia.

Author's Note

Although this story is about a real person, the artist Emily Carr, who lived from 1871 to 1945, it is fiction. My main sources for Emily's experiences are her own descriptions of episodes in her childhood, which are found in her books, *Growing Pains: an Autobiography* (Irwin, 1946) and *The Book of Small* (Irwin, 1942). In some cases I changed the order or timing of events to make them work together as a story (Emily Carr sometimes did this herself in her writing, so I don't think she would mind). I also invented some scenes and details to fill in gaps. I have tried to remain true to the spirit and character of Emily Carr and her life in early Victoria, British Columbia.

I will tell about the next years of Emily's life in *Emily's Dream*, due out in 2005.

Renné Benoit has been drawing pictures for a living for several years, a dream come true for her. For *Discovering Emily*, she researched the setting and characters with great care. Renée lives and works in Leamington, Ontario.

Illustrator's Note

The illustrations of the house and of the yard are from the actual house where Emily Carr grew up in Victoria, British Columbia, at 44 Carr Street (now 207 Government Street). The illustrations of Emily's family are also drawn from historical photographs.

Orca Young Readers

Orca Young Readers Series

Read more about Emily Carr's life in *Emily's Dream,* coming in spring 2005.

"Emily Carr, you get in this house this minute!" Dede's order rang across the cow yard. "Or do you expect your brother to take your punishment for you?"

Emily sat up, hay cascading off her. Through a hole between the boards in the side of the loft, she could see Dede standing on the back porch of the house. Richard stood beside her, looking at his feet. Dede had a firm grip on his ear. Hay dust drifted up, and Emily sneezed.

Well, that was it. She'd have to go in. She couldn't leave Dick to take the punishment on his own. Playing tag had been Emily's idea, after all. Dede was so unfair.

Emily climbed slowly down the ladder from the loft. The family's old cow lingered by the barn door, waiting for Emily. Emily gave her an affectionate scratch on the head, took a deep breath, squared her shoulders and headed for the house.